For Shale and Ever. May you have enough challenges to keep life interesting and plenty of love to make it all worthwhile.

~Dad

Thanks to my friends for always supporting me.

~Mae Besom

WHAT DO YOU DO WITH A PROBLEM?

Written by Kobi Yamada ✣ Illustrated by Mae Besom

I don’t know how it happened,
but one day I had a problem.
I didn’t want it. I didn’t ask for it.
I rcally didn’t like having a problem,
but it was there.

"Why is it here? What does it want?
What do you do with a problem?" I thought.

I wanted to make it go away.

I shooed it. I scowled at it. I tried ignoring it.
But nothing worked.

I started to worry about my problem.

What if it swallows me up?

What if my problem sneaks up and gets me?

What if it takes away all of my things?

I worried *a lot*. I worried about what *would* happen.
I worried about what *could* happen. I worried about this
and worried about that.

And the more I worried, the bigger my problem became.

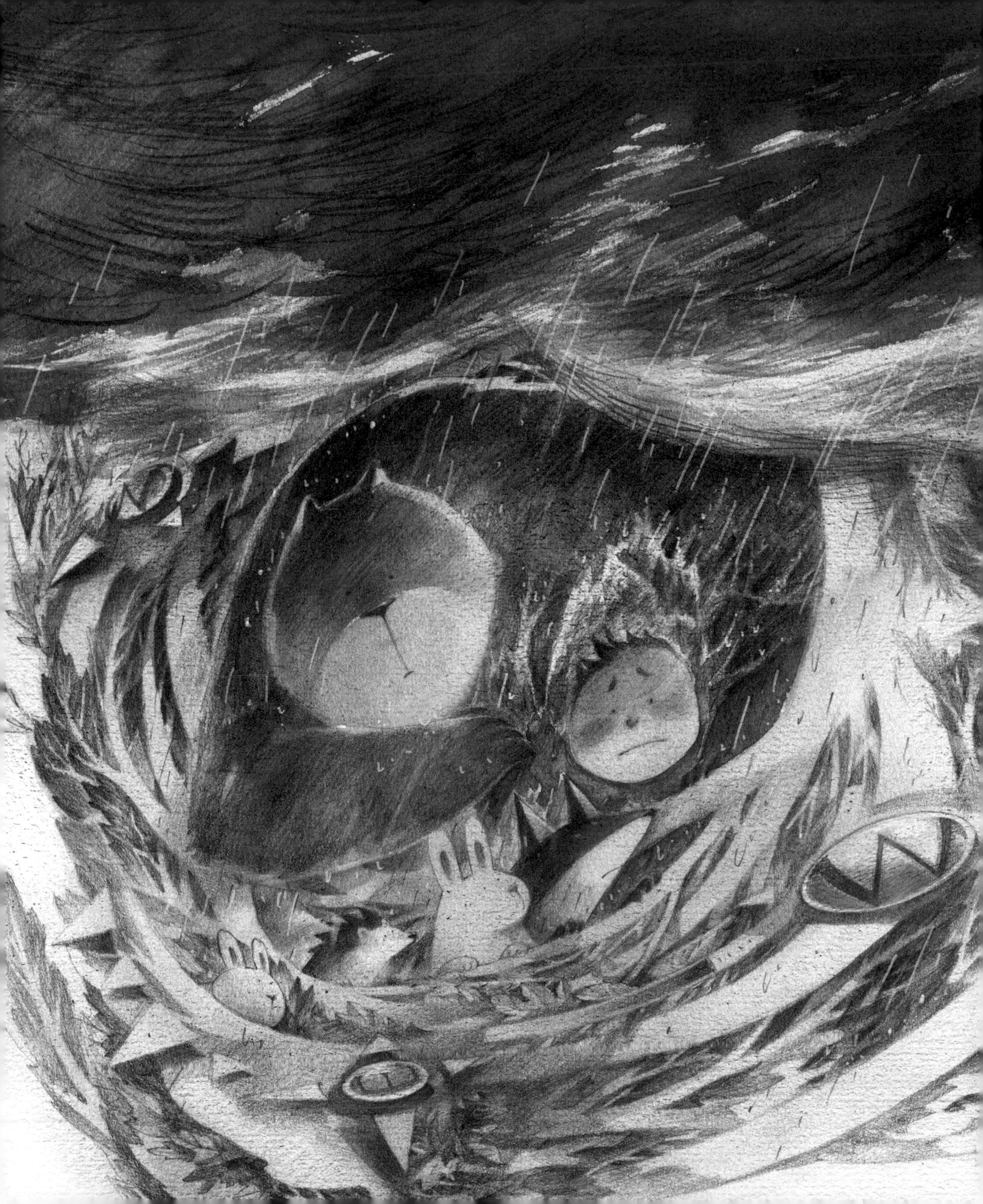

I wished it would just disappear. I tried everything I could to hide from it. I even found ways to disguise myself. But it still found me.

And the more I avoided my problem,
the more I saw it everywhere.

I thought about it all the time.
I didn't feel good at all.

I couldn't take it anymore. "This has to stop!" I declared.

Maybe I was making my problem bigger and scarier than it actually was. After all, my problem hadn't *really* swallowed me up or attacked me.

I realized that I had to face it.

So even though I didn't want to, even though I was really afraid, I got ready and I tackled my problem!

When I got face-to-face with it, I discovered something.
My problem wasn't what I thought it was.

I discovered it had something beautiful inside.

My problem held an opportunity!

It was an opportunity for me to learn and to grow.
To be brave. To do something.

It showed me that it was important to
look closely because some opportunities
only come once.

So now I see problems differently.
I'm not afraid of them anymore,
because I know their secret…

Every problem has an opportunity for something good. You just have to look for it.

WITH SPECIAL THANKS TO THE ENTIRE COMPENDIUM FAMILY.

CREDITS:

Written by: Kobi Yamada

Illustrated by: Mae Besom

Edited by: M.H. Clark, Kristin Eade, and Amelia Riedler

Design & Art Direction by: Sarah Forster

Library of Congress Control Number: 2015955981

ISBN: 978-1-943200-00-9

2nd printing. Printed in China with soy inks. A011605002

N
W